Daddy's Little Wordlings

Written and illustrated by Linh Nguyen-Ng

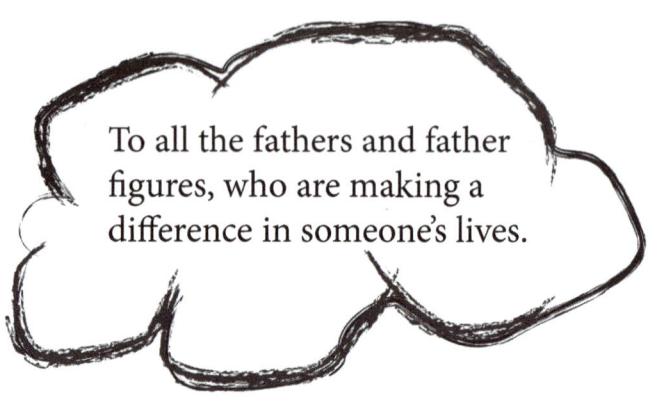

To all the fathers and father figures, who are making a difference in someone's lives.

Daddy's Little Wordlings
Text copyright © 2019 by Linh Nguyen-Ng
Illustrations copyright © 2019 by Linh Nguyen-Ng

All rights reserved. Published by Prose & Concepts LLC.
No part of this book may be reproduced or transmitted in any form or by any means, electronic, or mechanical, including photocopying, recording, or by any information storage and retrieval system without written permission from the publisher. For information:

Prose & Concepts LLC
210 Park Avenue, Suite #280
Worcester, MA 01609
www.proseandconcepts.com

This book is a work of fiction. All characters, places, names, and events are a product of the author's imagination. Any resemblance to events, locations, or persons alive or otherwise, is entirely coincidental.

First edition hardcover ISBN: 978-1-7323275-2-8
First edition paperback ISBN: 978-1-7323275-3-5

Daddy, you give me love.
It is bigger than the Earth.

I love catching happiness with you.

Your cooking is like a box of chocolates. I never know what I'm going to get. But I love them all.

When I was little, I wanted to be like you.
We were two of a kind.

You taught me some things are better left untouched.

Your hugs are safe like a teddy bear.

Your determination is brave like a soldier.

Your imagination is more magical than a wizard.

Because of you, I built dreams.

Because of you, I carved my mark.

You are my Super-Daddy, always chasing my fears away.

You gave me responsibilities. Those responsibilities grew into respect, dignity, and appreciation for myself and others.

Your words are precious coins in my Promise Jar.

Your presence is my umbrella.
You keep the storm away.

You are the flame on my Torch of Victory.

You are the "kick" to my sidekick.

You showed me the best tools to mend my broken heart.

You taught me that dreams take time.

You helped me pave my way to success.

I found my way because of your Map to Life.

I learned that an apology and owning my mistakes make you proud.

You taught me how to reach for the unimaginable.

You inspired me to be different.
My differences made me accept
who I am and be truly happy.

Daddy, I know you love me. But do you know how much I need and love you?

I need you the way a basketball needs a hoop.

I need you the way a train needs its tracks.

I love you the way a rainbow loves the rain.

I love you the way a book loves
its words and wisdom.

Linh Nguyen-Ng

Pronounced: (Lynn)   (New Yen)   (Ing)

I love the arts. I love writing and illustrating children's books because a child's world is so magical that I never want to leave it. I live in Massachusetts with my husband and two creative children. I love the four seasons because they inspire me with their changing beauty.
I'd love to hear from you. Connect with me below!

Website: www.linhnguyenng.com
Instagram: @landscaper.of.words
Twitter: @linhnguyenng
Facebook: www.facebook.com/lnguyenng
Mail:
Prose & Concepts
c/o Linh Nguyen-Ng
210 Park Avenue, Suite #280
Worcester, MA 01609

Join the Little Wordlings in more upcoming adventures...

CPSIA information can be obtained
at www.ICGtesting.com
Printed in the USA
BVHW021639030619
550004BV00019B/828/P